Welcome to ALADDIN QUIX!

If you are looking for fast, fun-to-read stories with colorful characters, lots of kid-friendly humor, easy-to-follow action, entertaining story lines, and lively illustrations, then **ALADDIN QUIX** is for you!

But wait, there's more!

If you're also looking for stories with tables of contents; word lists; about-the-book questions; 64, 80, or 96 pages; short chapters; short paragraphs; and large fonts, then **ALADDIN QUIX** is *definitely* for you!

ALADDIN QUIX: The next step between ready to reads and longer, more challenging chapter books, for readers five to eight years old.

Express Train to Trouble

Read more ALADDIN QUIX books!

Our Principal Is a Frog!
by Stephanie Calmenson

Our Principal Is a Wolf!
by Stephanie Calmenson

Royal Sweets 1: A Royal Rescue
by Helen Perelman

Royal Sweets 2: Sugar Secrets
by Helen Perelman

A Miss Mallard Mystery: Texas Trail to Calamity
by Robert Quackenbush

A Miss Mallard Mystery: Dig to Disaster
by Robert Quackenbush

A Miss Mallard Mystery: Stairway to Doom
by Robert Quackenbush

A Miss Mallard Mystery

EXPRESS TRAIN TO TROUBLE

ROBERT QUACKENBUSH

ALADDIN QUIX

New York   London   Toronto   Sydney   New Delhi

ALADDIN QUIX
Simon & Schuster Children's Publishing Division
1230 Avenue of the Americas, New York, New York 10020
This Aladdin QUIX hardcover edition September 2018
Copyright © 1981 by Robert Quackenbush
Also available in an Aladdin QUIX paperback edition.
All rights reserved, including the right of reproduction in whole or in part in any form.
ALADDIN and the related marks and colophon are trademarks of Simon & Schuster, Inc.
For information about special discounts for bulk purchases, please contact
Simon & Schuster Special Sales at 1-866-506-1949 or business@simonandschuster.com.
The Simon & Schuster Speakers Bureau can bring authors to your live event. For more information or to book an event contact the Simon & Schuster Speakers Bureau at
1-866-248-3049 or visit our website at www.simonspeakers.com.
Series and jacket designed by Nina Simoneaux
Interior designed by Tiara Iandiorio
The illustrations for this book were rendered in pen and ink and wash.
The text of this book was set in Archer Medium.
Manufactured in the United States of America 0818 FFG
2 4 6 8 10 9 7 5 3 1
The Library of Congress has cataloged a previous edition as follows:
Quackenbush, Robert M. / Express train to trouble.
Summary: When troublesome George Ruddy Duck disappears on the express train to Cairo, Miss Mallard applies her detective genius to find out what happened and save the reputation of the train.
[1. Ducks—Fiction. 2. Mystery and detective stories.] I. Title.
PZ7.Q16Ex 1981 [E] 82-8477 AACR2
ISBN 978-1-5344-1403-7 (hc)
ISBN 978-1-5344-1402-0 (pbk)
ISBN 978-1-5344-1404-4 (eBook)

For Piet and Margie,

and now for Emma and Aidan

Cast of Characters

Miss Mallard: World-famous ducktective

Sir Reginald Baldpate: Train passenger on the Valley of the Kings tour

Lady Teal: Train passenger on the Valley of the Kings tour

George Ruddy Duck: Practical joker on the Valley of the Kings tour

Professor Bufflehead: Archaeologist who found the ancient Tut-n-Quacken mummy case

porter: Train employee who assists passengers

conductor: Train employee who is in charge of the train and who sells tickets and collects fares

What's in Miss Mallard's Bag?

Miss Mallard has many detective tools she brings with her on her adventures around the world.

In her knitting bag she usually has:

- Newspaper clippings
- Knitting needles and yarn
- A magnifying glass
- A flashlight
- A mirror
- A travel guide
- Chocolates for her nephew

Contents

1

A Train Trickster

At breakfast on the luxurious Nile Express, **chaos** broke out in the dining car. The world-famous ducktective, **Miss Mallard**, could not believe her eyes.

Vinegar in **Sir Reginald**

Baldpate's tea caused him to spit it out and explode in a coughing fit.

A trick glass spilled orange juice all over **Lady Teal**'s dress, which had diamond buttons.

"**George Ruddy Duck** again!" sighed Miss Mallard.

George Ruddy Duck had been bothering everyone on the Valley of the Kings tour with his practical jokes. Sir Reginald Baldpate and Lady Teal had been especially annoyed by his pranks.

Miss Mallard studied Ruddy Duck as he came down the aisle laughing loudly. Suddenly he stopped at a new passenger's table.

Without warning, Ruddy Duck slapped the passenger on the back and sent his eyeglass flying.

"Hi, pal!" Ruddy Duck shouted. **"Long time no see!"**

"I am *not* your pal," said the new passenger. "And I don't even know you. I am **Professor Bufflehead**."

Ruddy Duck gave the professor another slap on the back. The

sudden blow made the professor choke on a piece of toast.

With that, Ruddy Duck left the dining car.

Poor Professor Bufflehead was still coughing and **spluttering**. Miss Mallard grabbed her knitting bag, which contained detective equipment. She went to help the professor.

Tossing the bag on an empty chair at his table, she reached for a glass of water.

"Drink this," she said as

she held the glass to the professor's beak.

The professor took a drink and stopped coughing.

"Oh my, that dreadful Mr. Ruddy Duck," said Miss Mallard. "He has nearly ruined this trip for everyone. Are you feeling better, Professor?"

The professor nodded.

Miss Mallard sat down across from him and said, "I've been most **anxious** to talk to you, Professor. I'm Margery Mallard. I joined the

tour three days ago for a holiday. I saw you come aboard last night with your recent discovery—the ancient Tut-n-Quacken mummy case. All that gold!"

She added, **"How very thrilling!"**

"Quite," said the professor.

"I hope you keep your compartment door locked. The treasure must be very valuable," said Miss Mallard.

"Quite," said the professor.

"I've read everything about

you," said Miss Mallard. "Your work is most exciting."

"Quite," said the professor.

"Some of it must be dangerous," Miss Mallard went on.

"Quite," said the professor.

"I read in the newspapers last year that you were injured during an important mission in East Africa," said Miss Mallard. "May I ask what happened?"

The professor got up from his chair and said **abruptly**, "Tigers chased me."

"Indeed!" said Miss Mallard.

"Excuse me," said the professor as he left the table.

"Oh, Professor," Miss Mallard called after him, "you forgot your cane."

The professor returned to the table.

"Quite," he said.

Then he **hobbled** out of the dining car.

2

Muffled Voices

That afternoon the train made a one-hour mail stop while **cargo** was unloaded.

A few of the passengers decided to go for a short camel ride to the pyramids.

The adventurers were Miss Mallard, Lady Teal, Sir Reginald, and—to the dismay of the others—George Ruddy Duck.

And when they climbed up on the camels, trouble started. Ruddy Duck offered Lady Teal a lemon drop as a peace offering. When she reached into the package, her wing was pinched by a tiny trap.

At the same time, Sir Reginald sat on a trick pillow called a whoopee cushion, which let out a noisy *FRAMP!*

George Ruddy Duck laughed.

"You'll pay for this, Ruddy Duck!" shouted Sir Reginald.

The sun beat down as they rode to the pyramids, making them very thirsty. Sir Reginald and Lady Teal began to drink from their **canteens**. When they tasted the water, they spat it out.

"Someone put salt in my water!" cried Lady Teal.

"Mine too!" hollered Sir Reginald.

The two of them turned and

glared at George Ruddy Duck. He **smirked** back at them.

On the way back to the train, Miss Mallard closely watched every move the others made. Luckily, nothing happened.

At dinner Miss Mallard kept her eyes open, but still nothing happened. When she finished, she retired to her compartment, for it had been an exhausting day.

At ten o'clock she was awakened by a knock on the door of

the next compartment, which was Ruddy Duck's. Miss Mallard listened and heard some **muffled** shouting. *Boom!* A door slammed! Then all was quiet.

At eleven o'clock Miss Mallard was awakened again by a knock on Ruddy Duck's compartment door. There was more muffled shouting. *Boom!* Again the door slammed and then all was quiet.

At midnight Miss Mallard was awakened by still another knock

on Ruddy Duck's compartment door. But this time there was no shouting—only the sound of a muffled thud. Then all was quiet until morning.

3

Midnight Meeting

At dawn the **porter** came to rap on
Ruddy Duck's door for a wake-up
call. The door was open, and he
looked inside. The compartment
was a mess! Ruddy Duck was
nowhere to be seen.

The porter was sure something was wrong. He ran to get the **conductor**, and together they went to Miss Mallard's compartment.

"You are an expert in these matters," said the conductor.

"**Please!** Please find Ruddy Duck and save the **reputation** of the train. Nothing like this has ever happened before."

"I'll do the best I can," said Miss Mallard. "I hope Mr. Ruddy Duck is not a dead duck."

She quickly got dressed.

Grabbing her knitting bag, she went to George Ruddy Duck's compartment.

She took a large magnifying glass from her bag and searched his messy compartment. She found a necktie and a diamond button.

"Ruddy Duck's tie is not striped, and his jacket buttons are made of brass," she said to herself. **"Hmmm."**

Then she found Ruddy Duck's

date book. A page was torn out. She could see a faint **impression** of writing that had come through onto the page below.

She held the book up to the light and read:

MEET THE FAKER AT MIDNIGHT.

Miss Mallard rang the porter. She wrote down a list of names on a piece of paper and folded it. When the porter came, she handed him the folded paper.

"Let no one see this," she said to the porter. "**Summon** everyone on the list. Have them meet me in the observation car in a half hour."

The porter left, and Miss Mallard went to her compartment.

She dug through the clipping file she kept in her knitting bag. When she found the news clipping she wanted, she read it carefully.

"**Mmm, huh!** I thought so!" Miss Mallard said to herself.

She closed her knitting bag again and went to the observation car. Lady Teal, Sir Reginald Baldpate, Professor Bufflehead, the porter, and the conductor were all waiting for her.

4

Disappearing Act

"What is this about?" asked Sir Reginald. "Why are we here?"

Miss Mallard told them about the mysterious disappearance of George Ruddy Duck.

"It must have happened at

midnight," she said. "I heard sounds coming from his compartment until that time."

Lady Teal spoke up. "What does any of this have to do with us?" **"Everything!"** answered Miss Mallard. "Each of you had a reason for wanting George Ruddy Duck out of the way."

She turned to Sir Reginald Baldpate.

"Where were you last night between the hours of ten and midnight?" she asked.

"In my compartment sleeping," answered Sir Reginald.

"Then how do you account for the fact that one of your neckties was found in Ruddy Duck's compartment?" asked Miss Mallard.

Sir Reginald blushed.

Holding a shiny button, Miss Mallard turned to Lady Teal.

"And where were you, Lady Teal?" she asked.

"I was also in my compartment," answered Lady Teal, who then burst into tears.

The porter started to say something. Miss Mallard held up her wing to stop him.

"Then how, Lady Teal," asked Miss Mallard, "did one of your diamond buttons arrive in Ruddy Duck's compartment?"

"Leave Lady Teal alone!" shouted Sir Reginald. "All right, we were both in Ruddy Duck's compartment last night. I was there at ten o'clock to ask him to stop annoying me."

He continued, "Lady Teal was

there at eleven o'clock asking the same thing. Then we met in the club car for cocoa to soothe our **frazzled** nerves. We were there until twelve-thirty. I know because I looked at my watch."

"That's right!" said the porter. "I was there. I served them."

"Thank you," said Miss Mallard. "That gives me the proof I need."

Very quickly she turned to the professor and pulled at his mustache.

"**Owww!**" said the professor as his mustache came off.

"Just as I thought," cried Miss Mallard. "**A fake mustache!** And now we see, instead of the famous Professor Bufflehead, an **impostor**—the **notorious** Arnie the Swindler."

5

Swindler Snagged

"How did you know?" asked Arnie the Swindler.

Miss Mallard answered, "It was when you said that tigers chased you in East Africa. No real explorer would make a mistake like that.

Tigers live in Asia—not Africa."

Miss Mallard went on. "Then when you left the table without your cane, I was convinced, especially after I checked my clipping file. It is well known that Professor Bufflehead cannot even stand without his cane."

"So?" **sneered** Arnie the Swindler.

"So Ruddy Duck must have known you were a fake," answered Miss Mallard. "He seemed to know you from somewhere else. That's why you had to get rid of him—to keep your identity a secret. What did you do with him, you rascal?"

"You've got me!" said Arnie. "I met that pest a long time ago. He hasn't changed!"

He continued on. "I went to see him at midnight last night. I offered him money to keep quiet, but he wouldn't take it. **Boy, is he foolish!** I knocked him out and then hid him in the Tut-n-Quacken mummy case in my compartment."

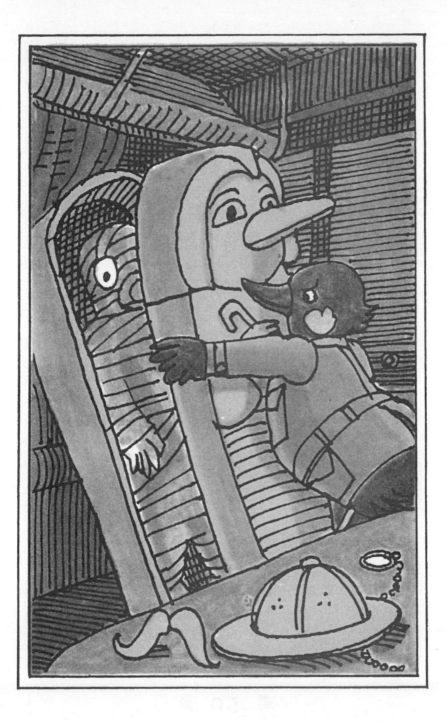

"And the real professor?" asked Miss Mallard.

"He's tied to a palm tree back at the digging site," answered Arnie. "I paid off the workers and stole the mummy case."

"Quick!" said Miss Mallard to the conductor. "Lock up this crook in the baggage car until the police can come for him. Then call for a search party to rescue Professor Bufflehead."

She turned to the porter.

"Listen very carefully. Go to the

crook's compartment," she said, "and unlock the door with your **passkey**. Let George Ruddy Duck out of the mummy case. **Now!**"

The porter ran ahead of the conductor and Arnie the Swindler. He soon returned with George Ruddy Duck, who was all wrapped up like a mummy.

"How can I ever thank you for saving me, Miss Mallard?" asked Ruddy Duck. "I'm so sorry now for all the jokes I played on every-one. I'll never do it again."

"So you've learned a good lesson, have you?" asked Miss Mallard.

"Yes," said Ruddy Duck. "And I mean it when I say I am sorry."

"Oh, that's perfectly all right, Ruddy Duck," said Sir Reginald as he placed a pillow on a chair. "Come and sit down over here."

FRAMP! went the pillow as Ruddy Duck sat down.

Everyone roared with laughter! It was Ruddy Duck's own whoopee cushion.

Word List

abruptly (uh·BRUHPT·ly):
Suddenly; unexpectedly

anxious (ANK·shus): Nervous,
worried something bad will happen

canteens (kan·TEENS): Small
containers used for carrying
water or other liquids

cargo (KAR·go): Goods that are
carried by train, plane, or another
vehicle

chaos (KAY·os): Confusion;
disorder

frazzled (FRA·zuld): Tired out; worn out

hobbled (HA·buld): Limped or walked with trouble

impostor (im·POS·tur): A faker; a person who pretends to be another person

impression (im·PRE·shun): An image left on a surface by applying pressure

muffled (MUF·fuld): Dulled or quieted

notorious (no·TOR·ee·us): Known for doing something bad

passkey (PASS·kee): Key to
a door of a private, restricted
room

reputation (rep·u·TAH·shun):
Opinion people have about
someone

smirked (SMERKD): Smiled in
a superior, puffed-up way

sneered (SNEERD): Smiled in a
mean way

spluttering (SPLUT·ter·ing):
Speaking quickly in anger
or making a series of short,
loud noises like the sounds of

someone who is struggling to
breathe

summon (SOME·un): To call
or order someone to come to
a place

Questions

1. Did you know that tigers don't live in East Africa? What animals do?
2. What did Miss Mallard take out of her bag to search Ruddy Duck's room? What two clues did she find?
3. If you could take a long trip on a train, where would you go?
4. Why were Ruddy Duck's pranks so annoying to everyone on the train?

Acknowledgments

My deepest thanks and appreciation go to Jon Anderson, president and publisher of Simon & Schuster Children's Books, and his talented team: Karen Nagel, editor; Karin Paprocki, art director; Tiara Iandiorio, designer; Katherine Devendorf, managing editor; Bernadette Flinn, production manager; Tricia Lin, assistant editor; and Richard Ackoon, executive coordinator;

for launching these incredible editions of my Miss Mallard Mystery books for today's young readers.

CHUCKLE YOUR WAY THROUGH THESE EASY-TO-READ ILLUSTRATED CHAPTER BOOKS!

EBOOK EDITIONS ALSO AVAILABLE